Harry and the Terrible Whatzit

BY DICK GACKENBACH

 Houghton Mifflin/Clarion Books/New York

FOR LILA, HELEN, ANNA, AND ARLENE

Third Printing

Houghton Mifflin/Clarion Books
52 Vanderbilt Avenue, New York, N.Y. 10017

Copyright © 1977 by Dick Gackenbach

Printed in the United States of America.

LIBRARY OF CONGRESS CATALOGING IN PUBLICATION DATA

Gackenbach, Dick   Harry and the terrible whatzit

"A Clarion book."

SUMMARY: When his mother goes to the cellar and doesn't return right
away, Harry goes down to search for her and confronts the terrible
two-headed Whatzit.
I. Title
PZ7.G117Har   [E]   76-40205   ISBN 0-395-28795-2

I knew
there was something terrible
down in the cellar.
I just knew, because
the cellar was dark and damp
and it smelled.

"Don't go down there,"
I told my mother.
"Why?" she asked.
"There is something terrible
down there."

"I have to go down
  in the cellar,"
  she said.
"We need a jar
  of pickles."

She never believes me!

I waited
and
waited
and
waited
at the
cellar door.
She never came back up.

Someone had to do something,
so I took a broom
and went down the cellar steps.
It was
very
black
and
gloomy.
And it smelled.

"I know there is something here,"
I called out.
"What did you do
with my mother?"

Then I saw it!
A double-headed,
three-clawed,
six-toed,
long-horned
Whatzit.

It was hiding
behind the furnace.

"Where is my mother?"
I asked it.
"The last time i saw your mother,"
the Whatzit said,
"she was over by the pickle jars, Runt."

I was sure the Whatzit was lying.
"What did you do with her?" I shouted,
and I gave it a swat with the broom.
WHAM!

That made the Whatzit really mad
and it came after me.

I swung the broom again. WHAM!
The Whatzit didn't like that at all.

It climbed up on the washer
and I hit it right where it sits down.

I noticed the Whatzit was getting smaller.
And when I pulled its tail,
it got even smaller.

Now the Whatzit was down to my size.
"Okay, you better tell me what you did
with my mother," I said. "Or else!"
"Kid, you're crazy," the Whatzit answered.
One of the heads made a face at me.

Just for that I twisted a nose,
and the Whatzit shrank some more.
"Why are you getting so small?"
I asked.

"Because you aren't afraid of me anymore," the Whatzit said.
"That always happens just when I'm beginning
to feel at home in a closet or a cellar."
The Whatzit looked very sad.

The Whatzit
got smaller and
smaller and smaller.
Just when it was
about the size of a peanut,
I called out,
"Try Sheldon Parker's cellar
next door.
He's afraid of everything."
"Thanks," I heard it say.
Then the Whatzit was gone.

The Whatzit disappeared
before it could tell me
what it had done
to my mother.
I looked in the washer.
She was not in there.

I looked
behind some boxes.
My mother
was not there either.

I looked
inside the wood bin.
No mother there.
I was very worried.

Then I found her glasses
beside the pickle jars.
But what had happened
to the rest of her?

I was searching
for more clues
when I discovered
the back cellar door
was open.

I looked
outside,
and there
in the
bright sunlight ...

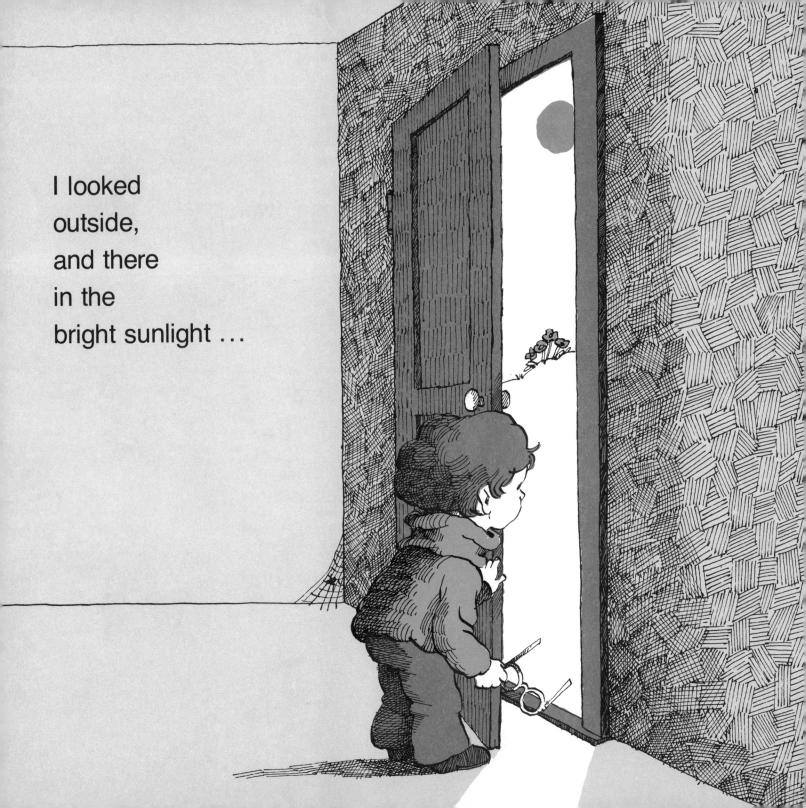

… was my mother picking flowers.
Boy, was I glad to see her.

"I found your glasses in the cellar,"
I said.
"Thank you, Harry," she said.
"But I thought you were afraid
of the cellar."
"Not anymore," I answered.
"The terrible Whatzit is gone.
I chased it away with the broom!"

"Well," she said, "*I* never saw a Whatzit down there."
She never believes me.

I helped her carry the pickles into the kitchen where she gave me some milk and cookies.

"You know what, Harry,"
my mother said.
"I will never worry about
a Whatzit as long as
you are around."
Maybe she did believe me.

Later I heard an awful yell
coming from the house next door.
I'll bet Sheldon looked in the cellar.

x